When I hated Jodi, I really hated Jodi. I binged, I purged, I ate, I didn't eat, I drank, I did drugs, I screamed, and I dulled the pain with whatever I thought would work for that second. Nothing worked. . . . It was not until I realized that everything I'd been searching for was with me all the time. This revelation did not happen in an hour, a day, a week, or a year. But somehow, as I learned to take care of myself—my whole self, mind, body, and spirit—the moment of transition slowly and lovingly crept up on me. Through grace, I learned about peace. It was more than a concept, it became a way of life.

—Jodi Levy, *The Healing Handbook*

THE
HEALING
HANDBOOK

A Beginner's Guide
and Journal to Meditation

J O D I   L E V Y

Pocket Books
New York London Toronto Sydney Tokyo Singapore

Although I make frequent references to women throughout this book, I'm
hoping that men will feel equally included and empowered.

POCKET BOOKS, a division of Simon & Schuster Inc.
1230 Avenue of the Americas, New York, NY 10020

ISBN: 0-671-02759-X

First Pocket Books trade paperback printing April 1999

10 9 8 7 6 5 4 3 2 1

POCKET and colophon are registered trademarks of
Simon & Schuster Inc.

Cover illustration and photograph by Rick Catalan
Text design by Laura Lindgren

Printed in the U.S.A.

CONTENTS

Acknowledgments   ix

Introduction   1
Music That Soothes Your Soul   5
Stress   7
The Healing Hands Stress Test   9
The Anti-Stress Declaration   17
The Anti-Stress Affirmation   18
How to Have a Really Good Morning   19
Morning Meditation   25
List of Simple Changes   26
How Are You, Really?   29
How Am I?   34
Record of Your Thoughts about What Needs
   Healing in Your Life   36
Declaration of How I Deserve to Be   37
The "How Am I?" Replacement Affirmation Theory   38
The Individual Affirmation   40
The Light Theory   41
The Light Affirmation   44
The Light Reflections   45
The Light Confirmation   46

The "Jodi Break" Experience   47

Afternoon Meditation   54

My "Time-out"   56

The Midday Affirmation   58

My Day, My Way   59

My Every Day   60

Creative Visualization   61

Visualization Affirmation   66

My Visualization Exercise   67

My Visualization Experience   68

Love—The Essence of Life   69

Love Letters   73

Bereavement   83

Preparation for Bereavement   87

Bereavement Meditation   88

The Cleansing Affirmation   89

Learning to Love   90

What's Love Got to Do with It? Everything!   92

Love Affirmation   93

The Levy Sisters   95

A Poem to My Sisters   97

Your Love Lists   98

Loving Yourself   101

I Am Affirmation   105

My Great Life—Now!   106

Laughter Lessons Learned and Lived   107

The Laughter Sheets   115

Laughter Affirmation 121

Fighting Fear 122

Facing Your Fears (I) 129

Fears Be Gone! 130

Examining My Fears 131

People I Can Discuss My Fears With 132

Facing Your Fears (II) 134

A Fearless Life 135

Life at Your Own Pace 136

The Fearless Affirmation 137

Just You 138

Honoring Myself with a Well-Earned Treat 139

The Perfect Day 141

When the Day Is Done 142

Evening Meditation 143

In the Evening 144

The Healing Hands Declaration of a
    Deserving Destiny 145

vii

ACKNOWLEDGMENTS

I would like to thank my sisters, Lori and Amy, for being a constant source of support. All of our challenges are always met with love.

I would like to thank Healing Hands' publicist, Mara Goodman, for sharing my vision, putting this all together, and aiding me on my mission.

I would like to thank my dad for his help and guidance.

I would like to acknowledge Gareth Esersky of the Carol Mann Agency, and Emily Bestler and Tracy Sherrod at Simon & Schuster for letting me reach so many.

I would like to thank the staff of Healing Hands and Elements of Life for working toward the greater good.

I would like to thank Elaine MacKenzie for her prayers.

I would like to thank Mark for his love, support, and companionship. You have renewed my belief in love and happiness.

Thanks to Ann Keating at Bloomingdale's for taking my vision and turning it into a reality. You'll always be my guiding light.

Thank you Richard Dixon for being the first one to take a gamble with Healing Hands; and for your patience, guidance, and constant inspiration.

Thank you Holly, Virginia, and Rick at Healing Hands for your dedication, creativity, and unlimited energy.

Thanks to Kimberly, Gabby, Juanita, and the irreplaceable Brandy at Healing Hands for your incredible teamwork.

I would also like to thank my mother, Dorris, for the gifts she has given me. I am with her always in loving spirit.

x

THE HEALING HANDBOOK

INTRODUCTION

I am glad that you have picked up this book and given me a chance to share my message with you. Although I am a young woman just approaching my thirtieth year, I have been given a full spectrum of experiences from which to learn and grow. Like so many women today, I've forged ahead in my career, walking the thin line between success and failure. I've had my every action and move accounted for in the business world. I've fought for principles and proposals, no matter how many challenges I faced—sometimes leading an army, sometimes being a soldier, and sometimes fighting the whole battle on my own. We've all been there.

I've won and lost in love ... sometimes in the same night. I've had to learn to let go of friends and lovers who brought out the worst in me, even though at the time I felt I couldn't breathe without them. This was a very difficult, challenging but crucial lesson to learn. The reason I allowed people into my life who gave me negative messages about myself was because on a deep level I believed I deserved unnecessary abuse. In order to really open myself up to the endless love and the boundless good energy source that belongs to all of us by universal right, I had to reteach myself to operate from a purely positive stream of consciousness. The first step forward was to come to grips with a harsh realization about the people who had bombarded me with pain and criticism. I discovered that my attackers were only passing on the anger and resentment they had not resolved within themselves. In turn, I permitted this negative energy exchange, until I finally understood that I am here in life to prosper, flourish, and live in a luminous light. Then it was time to move on.

My goal is to help you rekindle the effervescent glow of spiritual goodness and fortitude that burns within us all. I hope this book will allow you to reconnect with all the wondrous joy that awaits you here on this planet! To have all that is meant to be mine, I had to keep saying my affirmations and doing the exercises that you will find on the following pages, until I felt a shift in consciousness. And now that I am on a path toward mind, body, and spiritual wholeness, I use these helpful holistic devices to stay in tune with my inner self. I try to meet my daily challenges with exuberance and undaunted optimism. I also realize that being human means not being perfect. When I feel myself slipping back into a negative pattern of thought, I grab this book and lovingly remind myself of all the greatness I truly deserve.

Staying in a positive place of self-love is a constant, major, ongoing, relentless challenge. I have made it my life's mission to do it for myself and to bring as many people as I can along with me. I know self-destruction because I've been there. When I hated Jodi, I really hated Jodi. I binged, I purged, I ate, I didn't eat, I drank, I did drugs, I screamed, and I dulled the pain with whatever I thought would work for that second. Nothing worked.

The minute the temporary soul-numbing effects of the drugs, the booze, the food, and the abusive relationships wore off, I was left with a loneliness deeper than I could put into words. Five minutes seemed like five hours. I felt like no one understood what I was going through and nothing could fill up the huge hole inside of me.

When I began to make mind-body-spirit connections, I found that everything I'd been searching for was with me all the time. This revelation did not happen in an hour, a day, a week, or a year. But somehow, as I learned to take care of myself—my whole self, mind, body, and spirit—the moment of transition slowly and lovingly crept up on me. Through grace, I learned about peace. It was more than a concept, it became a way of life. Now the people in my life echo this loving choice. I am grateful for their supportive presence.

Perhaps the biggest hurdle that I had to face in my life was the death of my mother when I was turning twenty-one. Not having a mother's love, guidance, and support to guide me into adulthood was like losing my angel here on earth. How could a big, beautiful, bubbly

3

woman, so full of life, face away from an ugly, demeaning disease like breast cancer? I was shaken to my core without her, devastated by the loss. Although I will always miss her, I now realize that my mother still lives within my sisters and myself. In everything we do, there is a little bit of her. As I reconnected with myself, I reconnected with my mother. Although my emotional and mental pain has subsided, spiritually she and I have never been closer. I wish you, my reader, the same peace, the same reconnection with those you love, either here on earth, or in the spiritual world around us. I hope that by sharing with you some of the knowledge that was passed on to me, you achieve happiness, health, warmth, love, light, and anything you choose to make happen for yourself.

All the best,
Jodi Levy
Founder of Healing Hands

4

MUSIC THAT
SOOTHES YOUR SOUL

It is often said that music soothes the savage beast. Because I believe that stress has become the savage beast of modern times, I have included a list of gentle, relaxing music that has assisted me in my meditations. What music does is help me quietly slip into a more reflective state of mind, as I begin to connect slowly with the center of my being. Music has helped transport me from a place of crazy energy to a place of magnificent tranquility, when I needed to be really still. From this place of calm stillness, I began to clear away the clutter that had bungled my mind. I began to replace the negative messages that were clouding my head with a bright, positive, flowing stream of thought. I hope this list of music will help you set the stage for your own spiritual homecoming.

5

- *Healing Hands Mood Music*—by David Bryan
- *Watermark,* or anything by Enya—a massage therapist's favorite!
- *Anything by Yanni*—he is often referred to as the guru of New Age music
- Beethoven
- Bach

- ♦ Handel
- ♦ Mozart
- ♦ Anything from the above classics will completely clear your head!
- ♦ Anything by Enigma—a group that is often referred to as "The Jazzy Monks"
- ♦ Anything by Sade—an eighties classic who hasn't lost her smooth style
- ♦ *White Sands* by Andreas Wollenweider—a good introduction into the world of New Age music

STRESS

Stress! The silent killer of the nineties. We all have it in some form. Today's women are nothing short of Super-women, juggling career and family, trying to keep the peace in a chaotic world. As a woman's role in today's society becomes more complex than ever, so do the strains that attack her mind, body, and soul. Although we have the medical technology to detect diseases in their early stages and to administer treatments to fight them, the body's own immunological system is the most effective self-healer. Western medicine now recognizes that relaxation, stress reduction, and positive visualization are vital to the healing process.

I founded Healing Hands Massage Therapy and Holistic Health Care Company on the principle that natural prevention, taking care of the mind and the body in unison, is the best path toward optimum health. Stress was a devil I learned to fight with gentle, loving care. As soon as I learned to slow down and pay attention to the needs of my soul, serenity was mine at last.

This book contains visual imaging, positive thoughts, and insightful reflections of issues we all share as we go through the human experience. There are also places I encourage you to write down your own thoughts. I hope you will give yourself the gift of time to find a few uninterrupted moments to relax with this book. You deserve it. Enjoy.

8

THE HEALING HANDS
STRESS TEST

Stress is sneaky, in the way it seeps into our lives, sometimes making it difficult to identify its true cause. If you can identify the cause, the solution is not far away! However, sometimes it is not that simple. Sometimes it is a multitude of forces, both internal and external, that are the culprits in initiating personal stress. The culmination of these forces is tension buildup. The Healing Hands Stress Test is designed to help you pinpoint some of the major stress factors in your life. If you can deal with factors on an individual basis, learning to relax and handle them in a more peaceful manner, then you stand the best chance of reducing the negative effects of stress.

Take a moment to target your stressful challenges. Don't feel under any pressure to circle the "correct" answers. This is just meant to aid you in your journey toward achieving a calming sense of tranquility. Circle the answer that feels right for you.

1. Upon waking in the morning, you feel . . .
   a) refreshed, ready to start the day
   b) tired, needing more sleep

c) overwhelmed, wanting to pull the covers over your head and hide

2. As you perform your daily routine, you feel . . .
    a) happy; you get great pleasure out of what you do
    b) distracted; you're doing your duty, but your head is somewhere else
    c) anxious; you feel under the gun to get everything in on time

3. Your relationship with your partner is . . .
    a) a source of great joy, comfort, and support
    b) sometimes good, sometimes challenging, but overall, worth it
    c) draining, nerve-wracking; if you could only trust him/her; if only they would accept you as you are . . .

Answer this question if you are single.
4. My search to find a partner is . . .
    a) a joyous, fun, exciting process of discovery
    b) an adventure filled with twists and curves
    c) filled with upsets, rejection, hopelessness, and failure

5. Your relationship with children, parents, and family members is generally . . .
    a) good, loving, supportive

b) challenging at times, but overall we understand and accept each other, even when we disagree
c) awful, terrifying; just putting up with their presence is enough to make you want to explode

6. Your professional life is ...
a) creatively fulfilling, exciting, challenging in a positive way
b) exciting at times, difficult at times, but overall satisfying
c) boring, frustrating, beneath me ... just a way to pay the bills

7. Your belief about your own intelligence is ...
a) I'm a bright, creative person who is a quick study and a sharp shooter.
b) I'm as smart as most people, but don't really stand out in a crowd.
c) I often feel everyone is talking about something I don't understand. I can't compete. I have nothing worth offering. I have nothing worth saying.

8. Your belief about your physical appearance is ...
a) I'm an attractive, good-looking, desirable person. I've got great [eyes, hair, legs, etc.].
b) I'm OK—not a model or anything, but I'm not Frankenstein, either.
c) I'm too [unattractive, fat, short, dumpy, tall, ugly]. I'm embarrassed by the way I look.

9. Your belief about your personality is . . .
   a) I am a fun, exciting person to be around. People
      like me.
   b) I am not exactly the life of the party, but I'm no
      wallflower either.
   c) I'm a dreadful bore. Nobody finds me interesting. I
      better just shut up before I make a fool out of
      myself.

10. Your experience of life is . . .
    a) terrific! I'm learning something new every day.
    b) a roller coaster, but I can take the good with the
       bad.
    c) a nightmare. I'm drowning in my own sweat.
       Everywhere I look, there is a disaster I can't cope
       with.

11. When you sleep at night you feel . . .
    a) good, ready to rest
    b) like I need to unwind a little . . . but then I'm ready
       to doze off
    c) can't sleep . . . too restless. I toss and turn, try
       the TV, a radio, nothing works. I can't shut off.

12. When you feel anxious, stressed or overwhelmed, you . . .
    a) stop, take a breath, meditate . . . give yourself the
       time to regroup
    b) hit the gym, go running, swimming, or do any form
       of exercise

c) eat a whole pizza and a pint of ice cream, throw up, drink a bottle of tequila, take a narcotic sedative, call my ex-lover a thousand times and hang up, or hurt my body in some way

d) abuse others, physically or emotionally

13. Your biggest challenge in life is . . .
   a) staying positive
   b) losing weight
   c) making more money
   d) _____

Thank you for having the courage to answer these questions honestly. Now let's see how they can help. There is no secret method for tallying up a score. You don't get any spiritual or emotional "brownie points" for having all A's, B's, or C's. Most of us are a combination of all three letters. I'm sure one letter stands out in your answers more than the others.

If you have answered mostly A's, you are definitely heading in the right direction to becoming a happy, healthy human being. You are taking great strides to live your destiny to its fullest. If you really know that you deserve prosperity, fulfillment, and peace of mind, then I applaud you. This book will help you stay focused and affirm what you are learning to be true. Let these exercises, meditations, and affirmations reinforce your positive belief system and forward your spiritual growth. Enjoy the journey!

If you have answered mostly B's, you are just beginning to tap into your full potential. Don't be afraid; welcome your awakening! Forget the idea of having an overinflated ego or viewing yourself as conceited. If you reach out and embrace the "full you," you will only highlight all your best abilities. This book will help you make the breakthrough you are destined for! Really work these exercises and commit to the meaning of the affirmations.

When you walk through the world from a place of self-confidence, you will radiate a ray of hope to all you encounter. By "walking your talk," meaning living life according to your principles, values, goals, and dreams, you will serve as an inspiration to others. Instead of criticizing, others will see you as a beacon of hope if you have the courage to live out your dreams. Remember, we are not given dreams that we can't manifest into reality. Go for it!

If you have answered mostly C's, don't worry; I can tell you, this is where I was unconsciously living most of my life. I may not have had the awareness at the time to recognize it, but my deeply rooted destructive beliefs about myself were not so slowly destroying me. Believe me, I know it's hard to reprogram twenty, thirty, forty, fifty, sixty years or more of a negative self-belief system. It may even seem impossible, but the good news is, it's not! I also applaud you for having the courage to take the first step in discovering your true, beautiful, whole, well-deserving self. I also applaud you for finding the strength to identify these unwanted feelings and having the will to go about changing them. The mere fact that you have come this far, to pick up a book like this, says to me that you know there's a lot more you are entitled to. It took me a long time to realize that the way I perceived myself and what I had allowed myself to accept as truth were ways of denying myself my right to a positive living experience. Once I began to really believe that *everybody* has a unique, creative, original contribution to make, I began to break down my barriers and get rid of stress. Stress originates from built-up negativity. I found that once I was able to embrace the parts of myself I used to run from, I could deal with life's challenges more effectively. Once I accepted that I was truly a worthwhile person, I was no longer afraid to ask for help if I needed it. Asking became a source of strength for me, not weakness. The more comfortable I felt with *me*, the more manageable my life became. When stress popped its ugly head up, I had the tools and confidence to combat it, without hurting myself anymore.

How did I finally come to achieve self-acceptance? I started with simple meditations and affirmations that slowly but surely began to wash away the old negative *untruths!* I began to replace ideas like "I'm fat" and "I'm ugly" with "I'm committed to taking care of myself" and "My true beauty shines from within. How could I not be gorgeous?"

These little changes in my everyday thought process resulted in profound changes in my life. When I became my own cheerleader, my own support system, I finally became the person who was buried deep inside me, underneath a pile of garbage. I always thought other people deserved love, other people deserved success, and other people's lives deserved to work. Mine was doomed to be a mess. This thinking not only was the underlying source of stress in my life, but when stressful situations presented themselves, I would crumble under pressure. No more!

I urge you to start to reverse your thought process by saying the affirmations on the following pages. Don't cheat yourself by just mouthing the words. Allow yourself to believe each and every word of them. You can also create your own affirmations, once you get comfortable with the process. As you do these simple affirmations, you may be surprised at the emotional reaction you have. It's OK to cry or laugh, or have a reaction you may think is inappropriate. No reaction is wrong. Sometimes when you reconnect with the part of you that's been lost at sea, it can be a highly emotional reunion! That's the first big step on the personal evolutionary journey. Go ahead—laugh, cry, shout. Let yourself revel in the reawakening of your soul and watch the stress not-so-miraculously melt away!

THE ANTI-STRESS DECLARATION

I declare that anything
Or anyone
Not benefiting my ultimate good
Will not enter my realm of beliefs.
For my being is filled with good and plenty.
Only people and situations that fortify my wellness
Are allowed in my wonderful deserving space.
I graciously welcome
All that is waiting for me to embrace
And I simply walk away.
From anything or anyone that doesn't enhance my
incredible purpose.
There is nothing that is bigger than
My source of love, peace, and well-being.
I only dance with partners
Who don't step on my feet.
I only visit places.
That are as great as the castles of my heart.
I only open my window
To let the light shine through
Though it may rain around me
I am a bright, sunny reminder
Of the endless surprises
That are waiting to be discovered. . .
Inside ourselves.

JODI LEVY

THE ANTI-STRESS AFFIRMATION

I am an exuberant creation of love and synchronicity
My absolute perfection
Shines through my imperfection
Making me a glorious ray of hope
For all who encounter my welcoming presence
I have been lovingly granted
The strength and the will
To handle life's challenges
With complete effortless ease
Creating peace and flow of energy
To the working pattern
Of my life's natural design.
All is well in my world
As it was meant to be
Now and always
I deserve to reap the rewards
Of what has been sown for me with love.
Today and every day . . .
This is my truth.

18

HOW TO HAVE A
REALLY GOOD MORNING

I often find that how I wake up in the morning is a vital element in how I choose to spend the rest of my day. If I wake up with a negative feeling of unrest and a bitter energy, then that's what I will carry with me throughout the whole day. I know if I want positive things to happen to me and I want to create *only* positive situations, then I must start out on the right foot. Remember, from the very beginning, what we put into the world is what we eventually bring to ourselves.

19

What do we do when we wake up feeling like we wish we could crawl under the covers and give up? The first thing I like to remind myself is that every day I have the chance to start all over again. Every day I have the chance to have a new beginning. I am not trapped or suffocated by the events of yesterday, because today I can start creating exactly the life I want and deserve. Realizing that you are not a prisoner of the past is a very powerful, life-altering revelation. That does not mean you are not accountable for past actions, but it does mean you don't have to march into the present with a cloud over your head. The real beauty of morning is that it is the ultimate time for a rebirth or re-creation of yourself. When you wake up knowing that today is the first day, you can live your life just the way you've always dreamed. It is a lot more productive than waking up with a hangover from past history. That "I can't get out of bed" feeling comes from not realizing you control the events in your life. Change your attitude, change the outcome. Sounds too simple to be true? It's not, really. You just have to remember, when you wake up on the wrong side of the bed, *roll over!* Here are some easy things you can do to help you get your day off to the best possible start.

1. **Meditate.** As we are awakening, we are in the best state of consciousness to allow positive thought patterns to work their magic.

2. **Make love.** If you are in a good relationship, there is nothing more wonderful than a loving exchange with your partner to warm your body and soul.

3. **Play music.** As you shower and get dressed, why not play some relaxing music? Enya, Yanni, and David Bryan's *Healing Hands Mood Music* are some of my favorites. Put on any music that uplifts your spirits. Music does wonders for setting the mood of the day.

4. **Open the window.** If it is a nice day out, let there be as much light in the room as possible. Light is symbolic of happiness, and medical studies show

what people have known since the "dawn of time": it's hard to be depressed when the sun is shining. Morning also gives you a chance to appreciate and bond with your natural environment.

5. **Light a citrus or peppermint aromatherapeutic candle**. Remember, the sense of smell is very powerful. Citrus and peppermint naturally wake you up and put you in a positive frame of mind.

6. **Take a cool shower using eucalyptus or peppermint body cleansers**. The combination of cool water and these energizing elements awakens the skin cells, leaving you with that fresh, clean, tingling feeling. Because your skin feels refreshed, so will you.

7. **Eat a good breakfast**. You've heard your mother say it a million times, but properly fueling your body is important. When you eat a breakfast that is a nutritious combination of protein, complex carbohydrates, and fibers, your blood sugar stabilizes, keeping your energy level on an even keel.

8. **Exercise**. Exercise at any time is a crucial part of a total wellness plan. Those of us, like myself, who exercise in the morning like to start the day with an endorphin natural high. I also find that exercise in the morning keeps my adrenaline from working overtime later in the day. This kind of release rids

myself of any unwanted stress or tension I may be subconsciously hanging on to. The physical being must always work in conjunction with the emotional and spiritual.

9. **Walk a *dog* or feed a pet.** This simple act of nurturing allows you to bond in a basic way with a cherished loving being. Although animals may not have human intelligence, they are great healers in their own special way. Animals are wonderful sources of unconditional love and affection. A big silly grin on a puppy's face or the gentle purr of a kitten can be immensely soothing to a troubled soul. Pets reach us on a very deep level. They are often in tune with their master's real emotions. Never underestimate the healing wonders of the little creatures that are truly man's best friends.

10. **Make a list of simple, positive changes.** If every morning you write down little things you are going to do that day to create a positive experience, I promise you the experience will come. It could be as simple as "I'm going to smile at my coworker, the one that gives me dirty looks" or "If I get caught in traffic, I'm going to put on some soothing music or a CD of my favorite comedian, and just relax." I'm not saying change the world or change your life in one day or every day. Just make little, simple changes

that make your life a bit sweeter and a bit more comfortable. You'll be shocked at how much better you'll feel about the total picture of your life if you pay attention to details. You might also be amazed at how much nicer people's responses to you are.

I remember a funny little story that is such a perfect example of how an attitude change can affect the nature of a whole incident. I was driving on a busy freeway in Los Angeles. I had the radio blaring and I wasn't really paying attention to where I was going. I noticed that I almost missed my exit, so I skipped over a few lanes, cutting off several people. The last person I cut in front of was a guy in a blue van obviously in a rush to get to work. He was absolutely furious! He too got off the freeway at my exit and pulled up next to me at a stoplight. I tried to ignore him, but he rolled down his window and screamed several obscenities at me at the top of his lungs. I could sense that even though it was wrong to cut him off, his anger was far more deeply rooted than anything I'd done.

Instead of yelling back at him or just pulling away, I also rolled down my window, turned down my radio, looked him straight in the eye, and said, "I'm really sorry. Cutting you off was thoughtless and inconsiderate of me. I was just in too much of a hurry, like you are. I'm sorry if I upset you, I really didn't mean to. I hope you have a really great day."

All of a sudden, he stopped screaming. He looked at me. The light turned green, cars were honking at us to move, but he didn't. He then smiled at me and said, "I'm sorry I overreacted. I'm having a tough time at work. You have a great day, too. Be careful driving. I wouldn't want to see a nice person like you get hurt." We then both drove away.

This may not seem like a major incident or a life-changing drama, but in some ways it was. In a small way, I made a difference in someone's day as well as my own. He could continue on to face whatever challenges he had to at work, knowing there are still nice people left in this world, people who care. Also, I should be more careful and pay attention to my driving. I realized that for every car I was cutting off, there was a human being inside that car that I was upsetting. The incident made me not only a better driver, but a much more conscious person. I was lucky that I found the sense to appeal to the man I cut off on an honest level. My change in attitude made an otherwise negative, stress-building, morning-rush-hour situation into a positive human experience. Just a little change goes a long way!

On the next page is a morning meditation and a simple change list. Use these tools to give yourself the kind of beginning that will start your day in a fruitful, bountiful way.

MORNING MEDITATION

When you get out of bed, before you start your daily routine, reflect on this meditation. The following words will help you go forth into your day in the best possible light:

Good Morning . . .
It *is* a good morning!
And all is well in my world.
I greet the new day with joy and expectation
of all the wonder and glory
I have the power to create for myself today.
My possibilities are limitless . . .
There is so much for me to achieve . . .
With earnestness and
Vibrant exuberance
I venture forth into a welcoming Universe!
It is a Good Morning.
And the world waits for me.

25

LIST OF SIMPLE CHANGES

I recommend only two a week for the first month. Focus on making these changes a natural part of your daily routine.

Week One—The positive changes I will make for this week are:

1.

2.

At the end of the week, the results I have seen because of my changes are:

1.

2.

Week Two—The positive changes I will make for this week are:

1.

2.

At the end of the week the results I have seen because of my changes are:

1.

2.

Week Three—The positive changes I will make for this week are:

1.

2.

At the end of the week the results I have seen because of my changes are:

1.

2.

Week Four—The positive changes I will make for this week are:

1.

2.

At the end of the week the results I have seen because of my changes are:

1.

2.

At the end of one month you will have successfully made eight little changes. This is more than some people do in a lifetime! These positive changes are simple, almost effortless ways to improve the quality of your daily existence. The minute I started incorporating little changes like being pleasant to telephone operators, saying hello to the doorman of my building instead of rushing past him, and smiling at people I walk by in the street, I noticed my life was a happier place to be. Everything I needed to make my life work came from inside me. Once I stopped blaming people, events, past relationships, my parents, the weather, whatever, for my own misery, I began to create the world I want to live in. In Jodi's world, I get to choose and rechoose what goes on at every moment. I get to determine how I'm going to react to negativity. I know I have the choice not to let it in. I also have the choice to replace anything harmful or harsh with good, loving kindness. Once I really understood that indeed I was in control of painting the picture on the canvas of my life . . . I began to express myself with vibrant colors! It's all there for you to create, each day, as the sun rises.

HOW ARE YOU, REALLY?

Before I could start to reshape my life, I had to be totally honest with myself about what was going on, how I was truly feeling, and what it was that I was so intensely lacking. This was not easy. Being honest with oneself often forces us to take a look at things, feelings, thoughts, and emotions we have kept buried for a long time. The good news is, identifying your feelings may be a little uncomfortable at first, but it definitely won't kill you. Masking your true emotions or blocking them out by abusing anything—food, drugs, alcohol, yourself—might be the death of you, spiritually or even physically. It is so easy to forget that the body and soul act as one living unit. Because you can see your body and not your soul doesn't mean you don't need to nurture the needs of both equally. Anyone who has ever been in love, won an honor for any kind of achievement, or held a new baby in their arms, has felt a terrific sense of soul gratification that can't always be described in words.

This is why it is important to discover the whole spectrum of your emotions. This spectrum is a lot wider than most of us have really allowed ourselves to delve into. I remember how I used to feel when I first started getting massage therapy on a regular basis. Sometimes after a deep tissue massage I'd find myself in a flood of tears. I'd be embarrassed in front of the therapist. I'd run into the bathroom and lock the door. Luckily for me, the therapist understood what has happening to me even though I didn't. He or she would quietly leave my apartment while I got in touch with parts of my soul that had been opened up by the intense body work. I cannot state enough times how important it is to recognize that the body and soul work together. When you bury or deny your emotions and feelings, they don't just disappear into the air. What I experienced is that they hide deep in your body and slowly destroy you, unless you let them out. It is not until you recognize them and release them that they no longer have any power over you. It has been proven that emotional suppression has led to physical disease, time and time again. Western medicine is just beginning to accept what Eastern philosophy has known as dogmatic truth about the mind-body-spirit connection. The everyday expression "sound mind, sound body" simplifies a crucial concept in undergoing a total healing.

I used to suffer panic attacks in my early and mid-twenties. Anyone who has ever suffered panic attacks knows the terrifying feelings of helplessness, fear, death, and "out-of-controlness" that go along with the experience. Your heart races, you feel dizzy, you can't breathe, you are absolutely convinced you are going to die right there. What is going on? A panic attack is the physical manifestation or "somatization" (physicalized emotion) of your hidden worries and fears making themselves known through your body. When you turn a deaf ear to your emotional needs, do things that go against your gut intuition, or partake in situations that are potentially harmful to you, your soul has to have a way of getting your undivided attention! What better way to get you to listen up than to traumatize your body? Your soul knows you won't ignore its cries for help if physically you feel paralyzed.

31

Massage therapy helped to unblock the places in my body that my emotions had wreaked havoc on. The act of healing touch allowed me to free myself up physically. This led to a tremendous emotional release. It is hard for me to write about the intensity of the actual experience. It was like being let out of an emotionally torturous prison that I had locked myself in and swallowed the key. I felt so much lighter. I moved easier. I slept like a baby and for the first time in years, the panic attacks went away without artificial help from a substance. The feeling of terminal hunger in the bottom of my stomach got filled up by eating normal amounts of healthy food. I started eating to nourish my body, not to suffocate my soul.

Aromatherapy helped make the massage experience my ultimate healing tool. I inhaled the natural scents of clary sage, peppermint, jasmine, citrus, ylang-ylang, rosewood, and eucalyptus. I was left with a sense of clarity that I had not known before. Having an aromatherapeutic candle burning as the massage therapist worked on me was an important part of the healing process. If you've never experienced the art of massage and aromatherapy, I suggest you give yourself that gift. It is a great way to begin your total healing journey. I learned that we have within ourselves the emotional and spiritual tools we need to heal our mind and souls in a completely natural way. On a spiritual level this revelation made my gratitude and wonder about the universe soar to new heights. Any feelings of loneliness I was harboring began to dissipate, as I realized how perfect the workings of the world really are. Believe me, it was not easy for someone like me from the instant coffee-gotta-have-it-yesterday-microwave-thirty minutes-or-less generation to imagine myself benefiting from an ancient form of healing. However, the more I delved into the art of aromatherapeutic massage, the more I realized this was the key that opened the door to my personal evolution. As my body and soul really began to relax, I discovered the savior I was searching for was inside myself.

These are some of the reasons "How are you?" is such an important question. People trivialize "How are you?" When they ask, they're usually using the phrase only as a polite, casual greeting, hoping your answer will be "I'm fine." Actually, "How are you?" is a more inclusive question that people usually ignore to avoid sounding like a complainer. Think of how badly we wished we hadn't asked "How are you?" when someone gave an honest, detailed, personal answer.

Wouldn't it be great if someone asked, "How are you?" and you could answer "I'm great!" and really mean it? Why don't you ask yourself "How are you?" and see what happens?

Use the next page to answer that question. Write down any thoughts that come to your mind. As you assess your current state of being, realize there are no boundaries or limits. This can cover any area of your life. Be gentle with yourself, and give your feelings the acknowledgment they deserve. Remember, awareness is a big step on the climb up to inner freedom. Don't be afraid, the view is incredible from up here!

HOW AM I?

Circle your first choice. Try not to think here. Your first instinct is usually right on target.

HEALTH:
    I feel fit and healthy.
    I feel tired and weak.
    I feel OK . . . could be better.
    If I could change something about my health, it
       would be _____.

34

WORK:
    I am happy with my choice of work.
    I am not happy with my choice of work.
    Work is OK, it pays the bills, but I don't feel charged
       or stimulated.
    If I could change something about my work, it would
       be _____.

RELATIONSHIPS:
    I am happy with the relationships in my life.
    I am not happy with the relationships in my life.
    The relationships in my life are OK, but could be
       better.

If I could change something about the relationships in my life, it would be_____.

These are the three general areas within which most people choose to define themselves. On the next page, get specific about *how* you choose to define yourself in these areas. Before we can begin to heal, we must have the courage to recognize what stands in our way. Remember, the body and soul work as one.

It's not easy to take stock of ourselves, especially since so much of our survival skills have been based on suppressing who we really are.

However, it is the brave ones, the ones who seek truth and aren't afraid to hold a mirror up to their lives who benefit the most as their journey moves forward.

Now that you've taken a cherished moment to take a private evaluation of your life's events and state of wellness, the healing can begin.

When the body meets the soul after many years have passed—oh, what a beautiful homecoming that day will be.

RECORD OF YOUR
THOUGHTS ABOUT WHAT
NEEDS HEALING IN YOUR LIFE

Use this space to write down your personal healing diary.

DECLARATION
OF HOW I DESERVE TO BE

I am a healthy, living, breathing individual
And all is well in my world
As it definitely should be
I feel the sun's enriching rays
Energize the healing power within me . . .
I release any pain or discomfort
That may stand in the way of wellness
And I send that pain
A beam of healing light
That washes it gently away
And removes it from my being
Restoring me to my rightful place of strength
For I am here to bask in the glow of
A moving, revitalizing universe
That wants me to live life
From a place of sheer exuberance.

THE "HOW AM I?" REPLACEMENT AFFIRMATION THEORY

As was previously mentioned, one of the powerful things we can do for ourselves is to replace old negative beliefs with new, affirming, positive ones. This simple exercise will start you thinking in the right direction. Try it, and you will see that you will begin not just to believe it, but you will own the complete glory of who you are!

38

REPLACE	with	AFFIRMATION
I don't feel good.		I need to take care of myself right now.
I'm ugly.		I'm beautiful in my uniqueness.
I'm fed up.		I need a relaxation break.
Nobody likes me.		My differences are what attracts people.
I'm stupid.		I'm curious to learn about things I don't know.
I don't fit in.		I'm an original!

I'm a failure.	I'm enjoying the process of discovering my gifts.
My spouse/partner abandoned me.	My spouse/partner was not ready to accept my greatness.
I hate my job.	I'm in the process of discovering what my life's work should be.
I hate my relatives and they hate me.	My family and I are discovering our differences and learning from them.
I never do anything right.	I have the courage to try to do many things. I'm brave enough to try.
I'm fat.	There's more of me to love.
I'm boring.	I'm a good listener.
I have nothing to say.	My silence is calming.
Nobody understands me.	I'm an intriguing mystery until people get to know me.

THE INDIVIDUAL AFFIRMATION

I am one of a kind.
There is only one spectacular me!
When I was made they broke the mold.
Nobody will ever again have what I have
Or be who I am.
Nobody will have my smile
Or the twinkle in my eyes.
Whoever walks on this earth
Will never walk like me.
I am a unique creation
Of total goodness and grace.
The ones who know me
Are lucky for that gift.
For I have made this world
A happier, lighter, and brighter
Place to be.
I am so very thankful
For the things that set me apart
From those who are around me.
I relish my personal distinction
For my face in the crowd
Is the only one
That will ever be me!
What a fabulous thing ...

THE LIGHT THEORY

Another way I have learned to connect with the spiritual side of myself is by studying what is known as the Light Theory.

Many major religions and people who seek a spiritual path learn about the power of the Light. The Light is a protective beam of energy that reconnects you, as a human being, with the ultimate universal energy source. You don't have to believe in God to call upon the Light— no religious affiliations are necessary. You just have to be open to the idea that we are all made up of energy that is part of a greater energy than ourselves. The origin of this greater energy is not important. We just need to know that when we reach out to it, it is there to shield us, protect us, and ultimately heal us. If you can grasp this notion, then you can begin to tap into the healing forces of nature that have always been there for you.

Welcome Home

The reason the Light Theory is such a useful tool for me is that it is spiritual, but it manifests itself as something I can visualize. In other words, it creates a healing picture for me in my mind. We as humans are used to experiencing something with our five senses (taste, touch, smell, hearing, sight). If we can translate spirituality, which is an abstract idea, into something tangible, doable, and comprehensible, we have a much better chance of making it work in our lives. Faith is a wonderful thing, but I found that when I was just getting started, it was really hard for me to "picture my soul" or "spiritual energy." That is why the Light Exercise is helpful. Even if you have never tapped into your spiritual nature, this exercise will open it right up for you. Now, I know you can't discover something if you can't understand it. That's OK! The good thing is you don't have to climb a mountain, grow a beard, be silent for forty days, or subsist on yogurt to achieve a level of healthy spirituality. You just have to be willing to explore what could become a source of unlimited strength and power. The Light Exercise is something everyone can start with and everyone can relate to. Don't be afraid to try it. I was very skeptical at first. However, as I began to apply it to the parts of myself that needed healing, it began to do wonders. Take it from someone who once thought meditation was only for people who ate alfalfa sprouts and drank wheat germ juice. This exercise really works!

Although there are many descriptions of exercises using the Light, Healing Hands utilizes this easy method, using a candle as a guide.

THE LIGHT EXERCISE

Sit comfortably in a quiet room and light a white candle. Turn the lights off, so that the only light in the room is that of the candle. Focus on the flame, and take a few deep breaths. Do not close your eyes. Stare at the flame until you can no longer fixate on it. Slowly close your eyes now. Keep breathing. As you breathe in and out, visualize the light from the flame going repeatedly in your nose and out of your mouth. Now, envision the Light from the top of your head washing through your body to the bottoms of your feet. When you have a clear picture of that image in your mind, magnify the Light in parts of your body that feel pain. Concentrate on sending it to these areas while bathing the rest of your body in the encompassing Light. The passage on the next page will help you focus. Say it when you are finished with the Light Exercise to complete the meditation.

THE LIGHT AFFIRMATION

I call upon the Light of the universe
To protect me from all that is working against
My naturally healthy body.
May the Light gently wash
All the pain and imbalance
From my [area of trouble].
I call upon the Light to restore me
To my rightful state of vitality.
With the strength of the Light
All is well again.
So be it.

44

THE LIGHT REFLECTIONS

On this page note your reflections on the Light Experience. What thoughts and feelings did you have while doing this exercise? How do you want the Light to help you feel in the future?

THE LIGHT CONFIRMATION

Since this may be the first time you have explored this form of body-spirit-energy involvement, it may take awhile to reap all the benefits of this kind of meditation. By incorporating the Light Exercise into your relaxation routine, you should begin to feel universal connection and the ultimate healing energy transform your imbalances. You will then be restored to a more sublime state of equilibrium.

46

The Light from above,
Covers me in love.
With love I glow,
The energy flows
Through my veins
Until I am well again.

THE "JODI BREAK" EXPERIENCE

I would like to take a moment now to talk about what happens to us around midday to late afternoon. As we now know, it's terrific to start your day off with spirit and energy. However, it often happens that we get busy at work or bogged down in the process of "doing life," and we can easily lose ourselves in the whirl of just existing.

Around my twenty-first birthday, I lost my mother to breast cancer. After her death, I moved to New York City to try to start a new life. It was my first time living away from my home town of Nashville. I was working as an executive assistant for the president of a big record label. I wanted desperately to prove that I was as smart, sharp, and on the ball as the New York City natives. Just because I spoke with a Southern accent didn't mean I was about to be left behind or pushed around. In my mind, I believed the ridiculous myth that New Yorkers thought they were at the top of the world, and everyone else was beneath them. The preconception made me promise myself that I wasn't ever going to be anything less than an absolutely perfect businesswoman as I was working my way to becoming a young record industry executive. I was going to be at every industry party. I was going to know all the right people and make them know me.

Life in the fast lane really began to take its toll on me. After going out all night and trying to stay on top of things in the office, I was on a quick road to disaster. By four in the afternoon, I was practically a zombie. I couldn't keep anything straight or get anything right, and I could barely concentrate. By pushing myself beyond my mental, physical, and emotional boundaries, I became my own worst enemy. Everything I was afraid of becoming, I slowly became. Something had to give or I was not going to make it.

When I finally discovered meditation and aroma-therapeutic massage and natural healing, as I mentioned before, I ultimately began to slow down and gained more constructive ways of functioning during the day. Even when I stopped destroying my body artificially and gave myself the proper amount of rest, I still noticed I had low energy in the afternoon. I discovered later this is quite a natural, normal thing for people to experience.

I found that even people who lead happy, well-balanced, well-adjusted lives sometimes felt overwhelmed and out of steam as the day went on. If you find yourself dragging in the latter portion of the day, don't worry. There is nothing wrong with you. We must remember that we are physical and spiritual beings that need mind and body refueling. We're not expected to run on empty! You wouldn't let your car run out of gas and leave you stranded in the middle of the highway. Why should we do the same with our bodies?

In England, at around four o'clock in the afternoon it is considered "teatime." Here in America, we have the afternoon coffee break, and our children often have an afternoon snack. There is a physical reason for this much-needed refueling period. On a nutritional level, I've learned that the metabolism runs much more effectively if it is kept as even as possible. Any major drops in blood sugar can result in lightheadedness, weakness, dizziness, even fainting in extreme cases. That is why it is always good to have a small snack between lunch and dinner. This way you never experience any drastic dips in energy and you can function productively throughout the entire day.

Since most people are comfortable with the idea of a coffee break to meet the requirements of the body, why not take the same kind of break to satisfy the needs of the soul? Since you now know the body and soul act as one, why take care of only half of the total you? Sounds silly, doesn't it? You wouldn't brush just your bottom teeth, comb one side of your hair, put on one shoe, or leave the house with just your top on. The soul is just as much a part of you as the rest of your being that you tend to every day.

Think of your coffee break. How much longer would it take you away from your work if you closed your eyes, took a few deep breaths, and silently repeated an affirmation or two? I'm not suggesting that you go into a deep meditation in your office, lie down on the floor, or sit cross-legged on a mat in the corner. The idea here is not to make a big production out of it, just take a moment to regroup and start afresh. I know what most of you might be thinking: "I don't have time! I'm on a deadline! I have to pick the kids up! Do the household chores! Talk to someone! Do something! Right NOW!"

Well, guess what? You'll be more effective at all those things and more if you give yourself a minute to relax and recharge. It's funny, isn't it? You are probably OK with giving everybody else hours of your time, your individual attention, and all your energy. When it comes to yourself, you probably are having a hard time justifying just five minutes. I know I couldn't do it at first. What if someone saw me? What if someone asked me what I was doing? What if someone didn't understand it and judged me as some kind of nutcase? Finally, I got so frazzled, I had to just take the chance and do it. I was sick of being dazed and confused with that overwhelmed feeling piling up on me. I was ready to change how I managed my reaction to extreme pressures that were beyond my control.

That is when I came up with the notion of the "Jodi break." The "Jodi break" is just what it sounds like—ten to twelve minutes just for me. If you can give yourself longer than that, terrific. Even if you give yourself five devoted minutes, it's better than ignoring yourself altogether. What does a "Jodi break" look like? What do I do during a "Jodi break"? Actually, the concept of "doing" something during this time is contradictory to its purpose. This time is really about just *being*, which is the first step to relaxing. When you say your affirmations or meditate on a positive thought during this time, it shouldn't feel like a "have to." It shouldn't feel like, "Oh, it's time to do my affirmations now, like it's time to do my homework." That really defeats the whole purpose. The affirmation or meditative thought is just there to guide you back inside yourself. It's not a penance. I don't promise a ticket to heaven if you say your affirmations. If saying an affirmation is a chore at first, don't say anything at all. Take the time to clear your mind, let whatever thoughts drift in and out, as long as they don't have to deal with work, kids, or what needs to be done for someone else. Remember, this time is for *you* and you alone.

If you can, go outside, or if it's bad weather, find a quiet area where no one will disturb you. (Taking a break while driving in your car doesn't count because you should be concentrating on the road.) During this time, if you are not yet ready for an affirmation, concentrate on absolutely nothing at all. When you get used to doing this and you reach a comfortable space, the affirmation will come. It's important to remember that while saying the affirmations, you don't have to be a drill sergeant and pound them into your head. This is not like learning the alphabet or memorizing a poem for the school play. The real beauty of the affirmations is that they are designed to provide you with gentle tranquility. Affirmations remind you that your life isn't just a pile of "have to's" for other people. Affirmations prevent you from getting lost in a drowning pattern. They lift you up out of the daily grind, and break up the monotony of the daily routine.

How many times have you heard someone say something like, "Another day, another disaster" or "Same stuff, different day," or "What's it all for anyway?" or "Stop the world, I want to get off"? These feelings of life being one big, never-ending circle of duty creates boredom and frustration. Boredom and frustration lead to tension, stress, and suppressed anger. These feelings can result in self-destructive behavior. I learned to stop in the middle of the craziness and remind myself that my life was about much more than just driving through my daily routine in order to survive. It was challenging, but I had to keep remembering what my goals were, what my dreams were and that my personal objectives didn't deserve to be lost in life's shuffle. This kind of self-affirming "time-out" has been my lifeboat that has kept the tide from pulling me under. Dive into yourself and you'll do a lot more in your life than just struggle to stay afloat.

53

AFTERNOON MEDITATION

The midday blues creep up on us, filling us with frustration and procrastination. We feel stuck and can't seem to move forward. What can we do to get out of the dumps? STOP, think about how the wonderful ideas and energy you had in the beginning of the day made you feel. Try to remember that only you decide when you're in over your head. Try to determine the best possible solution to your problem. If you realize that you are in control of your situation, then it is easier to move ahead with great vigor. Repeat this meditation and clear your mental path forward.

My day is my own.
And I make my world work.
Ahh . . . the bits and pieces
That I need to link together
To put my world into action
Are ready and available for me.
I have the power
To set the process in motion.
I am the cause
To create a powerful effect
On the people and environment

That circle around me.
Ahh ... that need to sail smoothly
And make great changes
Lies within the base of my soul.
I can make it happen today!

MY "TIME-OUT"

Right now, in the midst of the craziness, hurried frazzledness of my day, I give myself permission to call "TIME-OUT!" On this page make a "wish list" of all the wonderful things you want to create in your life. Today is the very day to make your dreams become reality, in your own special way.

1. My wish for creating good relationships in my life is

_____

and I'm allowing that to happen by

_____ .

2. My wish for creating prosperity in my life is

_____

and I'm allowing that to happen by

_____ .

3. My wish for creating good health is

_____

and I'm allowing that to happen by

_____ .

4. My wish for creating inner peace is

_____

and I'm allowing that to happen by

_____ .

56

5. My wish for fulfilling a specific dream of mine is

_____

and I'm allowing that to happen by

_____.

6. My wish for fulfilling my most deepest desire is

_____

and I'm allowing that to happen by

_____.

7. My wish for creating something that would make me really happy right now is

_____

and I'm allowing that to happen by

_____.

8. My wish for achieving personal growth is

_____

and I'm allowing that to happen by

_____.

9. My wish for this year is

_____

and I'm allowing that to happen by

_____.

10. My ultimate wish for my lifetime is

_____

and I'm allowing that to happen by

_____.

THE MIDDAY AFFIRMATION

I acknowledge that I have a purpose.
My life is too worthy
To be led away from
My loving grasp.
I am a powerful individual
Who matters in the most unique of ways.
My presence creates a vast difference
In the movements of life.
Everyone and everything around me
Is affected by my strength of will.
I acknowledge my right to hold my head up
Above the rough waters
And ride life's waves
With the lightness and laughter
Of a dolphin's smile.

MY DAY, MY WAY

On the next page, write down a brief outline of your daily routine. After you see it in writing, take a look and see how much time is your own. I would guess not much! Go over your schedule and see when you need your "time-out" most. After a while, you'll just give yourself the time naturally. Since we are conditioned to "scheduling," in the beginning it might help to set aside the few minutes you deserve.

Repeat this affirmation before you begin.

I am committed
To reconnecting with me.
I promise to give myself
Love and care
As I go through my day.
I will comfort and protect myself
The best way that I know how.
I won't ignore myself
As I tend to the needs of others.
I am aware that I am my best ally.
It is my right
To feel the sand between my toes,
Dig my hands in the earth's goodness,
And walk with the sun smiling at me
Now and always.

JODI LEVY

MY EVERY DAY

My Morning Looks Like:

Morning meditation and visualization

Morning time-out affirmation

My Afternoon Looks Like:

Afternoon time-out meditation and regrouping affirmation

My Evening Looks Like:

Bedtime relaxation, meditation, affirmation, and visualization

CREATIVE VISUALIZATION

Now that you have made a plan which I hope includes your well-deserved spiritual "time-outs," you should begin to feel more relaxed about handling all that you have chosen to take on. I believe that we create exactly what we want in life, and the challenges we are faced with are lessons we need to learn. On that note, I'd like to discover with you the process of "visualization." Shakti Gwain wrote a wonderful book entitled *Creative Visualization*, which opened up a whole new world for me. It was due to visualization that I was able to found Healing Hands Holistic Wellness Company, write this book, and get my life going in a terrific direction.

What exactly is visualization? It's the process of imagining what you want in your life and turning that into reality. Remember when you were a child in school? When the lessons would get long and boring, I would look out the window and dream about running through the woods, riding a pony, or playing on the beach with my friends. When I was a teenager, my daydreams would be about the prom, a new car, or going on a date with the cute boy sitting in front of me. The teacher would always ask me a question I couldn't answer because I was involved in my private world. "Stop daydreaming, Ms. Levy. Welcome back to algebra" was a statement I heard often. I'm sure most of you have had similar experiences.

What is daydreaming all about? It's a form of relaxation where we escape into the fantasy world we wish we lived in. What most of us don't realize is that if we believe our daydream or vision, we really do have the ability to make it happen. Anyone who has achieved fame, fortune, a good relationship, or anything that they felt was initially beyond their grasp did so because they believed they could. They envisioned themselves doing it, and they did not give up until they manifested it. Now we all don't need to be movie stars or megamoguls or attain great wealth to be happy and have a good life. I'm not suggesting that at all. What I am saying, though, is if you speak to anyone who has achieved something spectacular, out of the ordinary, or even made a simple dream come true, they will all tell you the same thing. They had a thought in their head, they committed themselves to it, and they allowed themselves to really believe it. If you talk to someone who says something like, "I always wanted to be a dancer, but I was too clumsy" or "I always wanted to write a book, but I never had time" you will notice a completely different energy level in that person than in the one who has lived their dream. What enables one person to create the life they want can leave another person totally dissatisfied. Is someone a born winner or a born loser? Is someone born under a lucky star and somebody else living under a curse? The answer to these questions boils down to bravery. Are you willing to believe in your dreams?

Sure, you can say the kid born to a drug-addicted mother on the streets of Harlem or Watts doesn't have the same opportunities as the rich kid born to parents from Park Avenue or Beverly Hills. What about the kid from Harlem who stays away from drugs and gangs and grows up to be a doctor, lawyer, or any type of successful professional? What about the rich kid who abuses drugs and drives his Porsche into the swimming pool? What I'm trying to say here is that no matter what our circumstances, our only fighting chance to have what we want in life is to *believe our vision.*

This is not as easy as it sounds. We are constantly being bombarded with negative messages telling us "we can't," "we shouldn't," "it's not possible," or "it's beyond you." Our friends and family may even ridicule us for expressing desires for what they think is beyond us, but the truth is they really don't know. It's always the ones who try to suppress us who are scared of making their own dreams come true. People who try to suppress others have usually learned to suppress themselves in order to avoid failure at all costs. If you surround yourself with positive people who support you in going for what you want, then all the better. I suggest that you don't waste one ounce of your precious energy arguing with or defending yourself against people who criticize your intention. For me it has been much more powerful to say something like "I'm sorry you don't share my vision" and move on.

How do you get what you want? This is how I recommend you start:

1. **Allow your mind to go.** Indulge yourself by painting a clear picture of yourself living out your wildest dreams. Are you on a yacht in Monte Carlo? Are you climbing Mt. Everest? Are you in a beautiful home surrounded by a loving spouse and family? Identify what it is that you really want and play it over and over again in your mind.

2. **Pay attention to detail.** What color green is the sea your boat is sailing on? How cold does the snow feel as you climb toward the top? How many children do you have? What do they look like?

3. Remove mental blockage. On the next page is a visualization affirmation I created to help combat feelings of self-doubt or disbelief. When I started thinking, "Oh, I can't possibly do that" or "Something that good could never happen to me," I stopped myself in my negative tracks and reinforced my self-love, sense of worthiness, and self-beliefs with the positive affirmation that follows.

VISUALIZATION AFFIRMATION

I see myself in green . . .
A gentle coolness that flows . . .
Refreshing and awakening
My soul's greater knowing
That I deserve the love,
The warmth, and the glow
That radiates goodness
Through every part of me.
I am as deserving as
A king in the castle,
A queen on the throne,
Or a goddess in the sky.
I am loved and cherished,
Connected and empowered
By the stream of endless energy
That welcomes my wildest wishes
And clears my limitless way
Up and over any boundaries
Free to have it all.
May my vision of something better
Manifest itself for the greatest good
Of all involved.

MY VISUALIZATION EXERCISE

Now that you've given yourself permission to create the life you've always dreamed, let the process begin! Just as you are awakening each morning, and right before you go to sleep are the best times to visualize. Still, you can do it any time of day or night, whenever you feel most relaxed. Get into a comfortable position in a quiet area where no one will disturb you. Close your eyes and breathe deeply. Now, just like when you were a child, imagine yourself being, doing, or having exactly what you want. Feel it, taste it, be there, ever-present in your own reality. If you do this enough, it will become clear to you how to create and manifest your vision. Nothing is impossible, nothing good is out of the question. The only part of visualization we have no power over is the control of others' actions or feelings. This is not about making somebody else do, say, or feel what you want them to. This is about creating a happy, healthy life situation that is the best for you and all those involved. Now that you understand, go ahead and see what comes to mind.

67

MY VISUALIZATION EXPERIENCE

On this page, record some of the things that you experienced during your visualization process. This will help you keep in touch with your goals and dreams. Clarity is yours!

LOVE—THE ESSENCE OF LIFE

Of course it is wonderful to delve into the depths of self-love, but to complete the human experience, we must learn about love for others. Love is both very complex and simple all at once. I think the greatest lesson I learned about love is that it is about acceptance, tolerance, and patience, *not control*. Much of our valuable time is wasted on trying to get somebody else to do, say, or feel something we want them to. A lot of our energy can be used up trying to make someone be somebody they weren't born to be. This is the love power struggle we all go through at one time or another. I'm not referring just to friends and lovers. This love power struggle also goes on in family relationships. Several theories of psychology teach that the power struggles that are unresolved in the family are re-created in love relationships with chosen partners. I found that to be very true in my own life. It wasn't until I could create loving relationships with myself and my family that I could do so with a partner. Because my mother had passed over into the spirit world, I had to make my peace with her through meditations, prayer, and unity letters. Unity letters help us to connect with loved ones who have passed. They are written to achieve unity between a spirit on this plane and one who exists in the cosmic currents of the universe. This process was a tremendous source of strength, comfort, and relief during my bereavement.

I know people who have such strained family relations, they feel that all is lost. I always urge people I know to try and find some redeeming quality in a family member and make peace. That doesn't have to mean dinner every week, but it can do wonders when a stressful relationship becomes healed. In extreme cases, where you may feel it is absolutely impossible or not in your best interest to mend a hurtful relationship with a family member, then you can do it by yourself, for yourself.

By writing letters to family members with whom you need to heal relationships, you have the freedom to express your deepest feelings. Since no one will see these letters except you, there is no one to judge you, and you are not restricted to doing "the right thing" to please other people. This is your opportunity to speak what has been bottled up inside you all your life. Writing these letters can be a very cathartic experience. When I wrote my letters to my mother after her death, it was a huge release of pain, anguish, and joy. I was left with a feeling of completion and connection with my mother's eternal spirit. The spiritual bond I have now formed with her, through my letter writing or "journaling," is stronger than ever.

This letter-writing exercise is not reserved just for family members. For any relationship in your life that needs healing, writing a letter can be very therapeutic. Whether you choose to send the letter or not is up to you, but that is not really the purpose of the exercise. This is about giving yourself a relationship clearing. It is similar to taking the garbage out of your emotional life. It doesn't serve you or the person involved to hang on to anger or resentment. Realistically, as in strained family situations, it is not always in your best interest "to kiss and make up," but it definitely does not do you any good to be weighed down by conflicts from the past. Sometimes in order to release and let go of a nightmare relationship you have to face it and confront it in a productive way (like writing a letter).

I find that when I keep emotions and feelings bottled up inside me, eventually I blow like a volcano! It has also been discovered in scientific studies that there is a direct correlation between concealing negative emotions and creating disease in the body. This is all part of the new integration of mind and body healing that Western medicine is finally coming to accept as valid. Eastern philosophies have based their healing principles on the mind-body connection since ancient times, as I previously mentioned.

The next few pages give you a chance to record everything you always wanted to say to family, friends, and lovers. Before we can attract people who bring out the best in us, it is always a beneficial step to put the past to rest. Remember, this is just for you. Speak from your soul and all will be well.

LOVE LETTERS

LETTER TO MOM

This is the woman who brought you into the world. She gave you the gift of life and did the best she could with the knowledge she had. Use this space to tell her all you need her to know.

73

LETTER TO MOM *(continued)*

LETTER TO DAD

Whether your father was a big part of your life, not there at all, or somewhere in between, we all have something we wish we could tell him.

75

LETTER TO DAD *(continued)*

LETTER TO A SIBLING

This page and the next are reserved for sharing thoughts and feelings with those people who were your best friends and worst enemies growing up. Let yourself define these relationships and put them in the right place deep in your heart.

LETTER TO A SIBLING *(continued)*

LETTER TO MY CHILDREN

If you have children, this is a space to share your hopes, dreams, and wishes for their wonderful future. This is especially good if you are caught in a power struggle with a teenager or are just getting to know a new baby.

LETTER TO MY CHILDREN *(continued)*

80

LETTER TO A LOVER

This space can be used to resolve a past or present situation with a romantic partner. Take advantage and "spill" all those "mushy, gushy" emotions you think are too corny to share! If you have suffered pain or disappointment, this is also a good place to write about it. Let it all out.

81

LETTER TO A LOVER *(continued)*

BEREAVEMENT

Once you've written these letters, you should begin to feel a sense of comfort and relief. It may even feel as if a big weight has been lifted. A heavy heart is a large load to carry.

A lesson we need to learn is that love is sometimes accompanied by loss. Learning to let go of someone you love can feel like hell on earth. For me, grieving and letting go were so painful at times, I felt as though I would die. Yet I lived through it. Whether it's the death of a parent or of a relationship, letting go is anything but easy. We naturally and instinctively are capable of making very deep attachments. When we are attracted to someone, it's a physical and emotional experience. We remember the sound of their laughter, the way their arms feel when they're wrapped around us, their smell, and the softness of their kiss. These impressions are imprinted on our souls. I remember reading in a college psychology course about the baby ducks who follow their mother around based on her scent. Every time I go near a pond and see baby ducks waddling faithfully behind their mother, I marvel at this miracle of natural attachment.

Often I would ask myself, "Why is it that nature programs us to form deep bonds with other people, only to have us eventually let go on some level?" I especially asked myself this question after my mother's death and again after the breakup of my relationship with a boyfriend.

Neither I nor anyone else can really have a definite answer for that question. What I can tell you is that for reasons that may be greater than we currently can grasp, *we need to experience the process of letting go.* It has also been made clear to me that if we don't get it the first time, guess what, we have to do it again and again until we fully realize that death is a part of love and a bigger part of life. This is a tough one! As a matter of fact, I can't think of anything harder, tougher, or more challenging than dealing with the loss of a loved one.

This led me to devise a system of dealing with loss. What I've tried to learn from living through my mother's death is to bond with her on a spiritual plane. I truly believe that even though her physical body is no longer here I can still connect with her on a higher level. Through quiet meditation, I feel that many times I have tapped into her energy. I've been able to reach her spirit and feel her liveliness once more. Please don't think I've been sitting with a Ouija board or conducting séances in my apartment. It's been nothing that extreme. In a simple, relaxed, meditative state, lying comfortably on my bed, I have felt Mom's presence and energy, reassuring and protecting me as she did when she was with me in her physical form. It was a loving experience. I encourage you all to try it, once you are completely at ease with some of the meditation and relaxation methods we have explored in this book. Connecting with Mom on a spiritual level has granted me a great source of love and hope. It has been life- and love-affirming, in the truest sense of the words.

The end of the relationship with my boyfriend was also very traumatic, although in a different way. We all expect to lose our parents (even though we can never be fully prepared emotionally when it happens), but I had high hopes that this romantic situation had a bright future. When things started to go wrong, I stuck my head in the sand and made all kinds of excuses. My fear of letting go held me captive to abusive behavior and total neglect. When things got to the point of no return, I had no choice but to drop my fear of letting go and get on with it.

This situation was also the death of a love and a profound dream. At the time I felt as if I would never love or be loved again. Eventually, however, I learned that it was up to me when I would allow myself to let love in my life. While healing, I began to realize that I have the ability to attract a loving relationship. Life is too short to waste crying over someone whose actions are out of my control. I realized that what I could control was how I was going to live the rest of my life, starting right NOW!

On the next few pages are a meditation and an affirmation that have helped me during difficult times. My message to you is that if you feel as if a part of you is dying, remember there is an even bigger part of you waiting to be reborn!

86

PREPARATION
FOR BEREAVEMENT

We don't always understand loss. When someone we love dies or leaves, it sometimes goes beyond our rational thinking. One of the things to do is accept that there are events in this universe that happen for a reason. We are all part of a loving universe. When it is time for us to leave and continue our journey on a different plane, then so be it. Even though my mom was sick for a long time, nothing could prepare me for how devastated I felt the day she died. The day Dorris Levy died, my whole world collapsed, yet I knew deep down I had to go on.

Grieving, crying, or any other safe, nondestructive way of expressing sadness is crucial to letting go. Eventually, peace of mind will find the way back into your life. Remember the wonderful times you shared with that person. Try also to talk about your feelings during this period—anger, loneliness—with a good friend or confidant.

The more we embrace the chance to grow spiritually through loss, the more we evolve toward our highest good. If we can keep this in mind while we are going through our heartache, we will come to know that love is just behind the next door.

BEREAVEMENT MEDITATION

I am a member of this universe.
I let love flow freely,
And know I am loved.
I trust that when it's time to let go
I can release my loss effortlessly.
I believe everything happens for a reason.
I know I will be refilled in my heart and soul,
Never empty, as my connections to this world
Will never leave me alone.
I am one with creation,
I release and let go.

THE CLEANSING AFFIRMATION

It is an important part of the healing process not to dwell on past or present negativity, whether it is emotional or physical. We must acknowledge negativity briefly, then release it swiftly in order to enhance positive aspects with grace and ease. It is our universal right to be happy and healthy.

The Cleansing Affirmation may be used at the beginning of each day, before a meditation, or anytime a crisis arises.

Sit quietly, in a calm, peaceful place. Take a few deep breaths and allow the following words to become a natural part of you.

I release with strength and will
anything that isn't moving me forward
toward my place of highest joy.
I welcome warmly into my heart
and I passionately embrace
all the goodness
that is meant for me in this life.
I am a valued member of this universe.
It is my right to thrive, prosper, and rejoice.
It is my right to enjoy the result of my work.
It is my right to strive for success.
I am exactly who I want to be,
Starting right now.

89

LEARNING TO LOVE

Now that we have begun to rid ourselves of negative relationships and have dealt with death, let's get back to what we are here to create ... Love! Love! Love! I really can't say it enough: we have been put on this earth to give and receive love. It is our right as individuals to have a life filled with love. I truly believe that love is a special gift from the universe. It is proof that we are a part of something greater than ourselves.

There are many ways of bringing love into your life. Of course, romantic love is the kind everybody dreams about. But there are many other dimensions of love that we sometimes underestimate. Love of a parent, sibling, friend, child, teacher, pet—nature can bring enriching fulfillment into your everyday life. I like to say that love is open for business 24 hours a day, 7 days a week, 365 days a year. That means that as long as we approach the people in our lives and the new people we encounter from a position of love, we can't lose. An act of love can be as simple as smiling at a stranger, giving a homeless person some change, calling your grandmother, or hugging a loved one. Think of what this world would be like if everyone treated everyone else with unconditional love. That may sound like a pipe dream. However, I found that once I substituted hostility, impatience, and intolerance with love, acceptance, and compassion, my world was an easier, lovelier place to live in. I wish that kind of transforming experience for all of you. Some say you find love when you least expect it. I say expect it, and get out there and make it happen!

WHAT'S LOVE GOT TO
DO WITH IT? EVERYTHING!

Love is desired by most people. We want it because we are
on this earth to have love. However, in order to have love,
we have to be love. How does one be love? A simple act of
kindness, a minimal gesture such as a smile sends love
out into the universe. Love has a wonderful boomerang
effect, too. The more we send out, the more we get back.
Can you remember the first time you felt love? Actually,
those of us who had loving families as babies didn't realize that our family's love kept us alive in our formative
years, but we all know how *good* and warm it felt.

If you feel there is a lack of love in your life, you can
do something about it. Forget magical potions, or so-
called love spells. It is much easier than that. Make a list
of all the people in your life that you love. It doesn't matter what kind of love it is: mother, husband, friend, child,
pet. Any kind of love is great. Write down what it is you
love about them most. After you've made this list, you
should already begin to feel love. Show the people the love
you now feel, by doing one act of kindness for them they
didn't expect. By acting out love, you will pull all the love in
the world directly to you. Watch and see. Love is a powerful action. *It works.*

LOVE AFFIRMATION

Look in the mirror and begin to welcome love into your life!

I am love.
I send love to all who know me.
Because of my love,
People feel happiness, plants grow, animals respond.
To any part of me that feels pain, I send love.
Because of my love,
I feel the love from others
radiate back toward me.
I am on this earth to act on love
and receive love in return.

JODI LEVY

It is the will of the universe
for me to surround myself in love.
Love is my right, to give, to be, to have.
I love the world. And
the world loves me.
So be it.

THE LEVY SISTERS

Almost all of us have people in our lives whom we love. Although we don't love everything about everyone all the time, usually when we love someone, the good outweighs the bad. If the bad outweighs the good, we must ask ourselves, "Is that person worthy of our love?" The Levy sisters—Jodi, Lori, and Amy—disagree all the time. We are three vibrant, strong, charismatic women with our own opinions, attitudes, and beliefs. We give each other the freedom to express our differences. As much as we may argue, the love and respect we have for each other is absolutely unconditional. No matter what we say or do, we continue to love and support each other. Love is an understood and powerful tie that holds us together through thick and thin. We know that it is safe to make our viewpoint known.

If an outsider attacks one of us, the other two will quickly rush to her defense, even if we just had a fight five minutes before. No matter what challenges life brings us, we face them together with love. We wish the same for you and your family!

Anybody who is in touch with family knows that it can be challenging at times to defend their faults. That is usually because if we are lucky enough to have an intimate relationship with family, we often take their good points for granted. I find that I can argue freely with my sisters because basically I love them no matter what. An outsider who attacks one of my sisters does not have that basis of love that I have for my own flesh and blood. This is an important thing to remember. The trick is to not become so familiar with your family that you lose that special love. If you hear someone insult your mother, father, sister, brother, or any member of your family, remember that person doesn't have your loving frame of reference. Even if you feel the insult is justified, I'd say defend your family publicly, then hash it out with them privately.

I don't believe that children should be held account-able for the sins of their fathers, or spouses should be guilty for each other's bad behavior. However, I think it is the ultimate sign of unconditional love if you can speak about a relative with forgiveness and understanding. Your display of family loyalty can soften even the harshest enemy's protests. True loyalty is a rare type of love, which we need to keep from becoming extinct.

A POEM TO MY SISTERS

We wear each other's clothes
and share each other's souls.
We clash like thunder
it is no small wonder.
The love and compassion we share
even as we pull each other's hair!
Although we can't resist a good fight
to the outside world, we always unite.
Jodi, Amy, and Lori
a sisterly love story.
We will always be together
and ride out all of life's stormy weather.
As we remember our mother
we are so grateful for each other . . .
And so we carry on
with the love that makes us strong.
We are sisters—spring, summer, winter, and fall.
We are sisters—that says it all.

JODI LEVY

YOUR LOVE LISTS

On the following pages list the people you love and what you love about them. This will help you take stock of all the goodness that already exists in your life. This list doesn't have to consist of romantic or familial love relationships. Don't forget best friends, teachers, even pets. Love is limitless.... The more you give, the more you get.

98

LOVE LIST

I Love: I Love Them Because:

LOVE LIST

I Love: I Love Them Because:

100

LOVING YOURSELF

Now that you've recorded the special qualities you love about the people in your life, think about what you love about yourself. You've heard it again and again: "You can't love someone else until you learn to love yourself." This is true because if you don't believe you are lovable, you can't allow someone to treat you well or appreciate your wonderful personality traits until you do.

We need to learn to view our faults with love, the same way we selectively overlook the negative aspects of others we choose to love. Show yourself the kind of love you would like to receive from others. This will help us to become more willing to share love with ourselves and the world around us. Love yourself first and you will discover that you have plenty left to give to others.

On the following pages, list what you love about yourself. Don't feel you are being conceited or self-centered. Everybody has attributes that make them lovable to themselves and others.

I LOVE MYSELF BECAUSE:

My best personality traits are:
1.
2.
3.
4.
5.

My best physical traits are:
1.
2.
3.
4.
5.

My good beliefs about myself are:
1.
2.
3.
4.
5.

Some of my best accomplishments are:

1.

2.

3.

4.

5.

Some good things people say about me are:

1.

2.

3.

4.

5.

Some of my hidden talents are:

1.

2.

3.

4.

5.

Some of the gifts I have to share in this lifetime are:

1.

2.

3.

4.

5.

I hope the love section of this book has had the biggest impact on you. The healing power of love is a universal gift. When you invite love into your life, small miracles occur every day!

It was the love of my family, friends, spiritual teachers, and holistic massage therapists that brought about my own healing. They were there for me all the time. All I needed was the courage to reach out to them. As challenging as rediscovering and relearning self-love is, it is worth every moment spent. Once I began to accept the total picture of who I am, I began to embrace it and celebrate! There is only one you, and the world needs your contribution. Never underestimate the power, the individuality, and the uniqueness of your place here on earth.

I AM AFFIRMATION

I am a gentle loving soul
who contains all the spectacular elements
of all things living.
Energy is the positive charge
I bring to every living creature
I meet.
Without me
there would be a missing part
in life's multitude of greatness.
I celebrate myself in all my endless glory.
My faults make me flawless.
I'm not afraid to say
I am a gift that should be opened
to the universe and all creation.

JODI LEVY

MY GREAT LIFE—NOW!

Now that you have begun to acknowledge your mind-body-spirit relationship, let's look at all the positive elements in the physical world that enhance the spirit. There is so much around us that distracts us from enjoyment. It is time to reintroduce ourselves to goodness as we sweep away the darkness.

Look deep into your life. Find the wonderful things in your life and fill yourself with them. By doing so, you're in the process of clearing away the negativity. Once you become open and accepting of love and the other positive aspects of life, you will see that you have these elements in abundance.

Use this space to take note of what is great in your life.

106

LAUGHTER LESSONS
LEARNED AND LIVED

Perhaps one of the biggest lessons I had to learn was about laughter, the greatest healer on earth. I've heard it said that the definition of resilience is turning tragedy into comedy. I often think that laughter is perhaps the universe's way of giving us eternal hope to deal with any crisis.

When my mom was in the hospital, my uncle used to call her with a new joke every day. Even though her body was traumatized with breast cancer, her effervescent spirit still bubbled over every time she let out her famous laugh. Sometimes, even now, when I hear a joke that I know she would have enjoyed, I could swear I hear her big, hearty laugh shaking up the heavens.

In the face of tragedy, physical or emotional, it always helps to find the lighter side. Obviously there is nothing humorous about my mother dying of breast cancer. However, it was her humor, her ability to keep smiling, that made her last days as enjoyable as possible. If I tell you that she died smiling, it wouldn't be far from the truth. At the time, it was hard for my sisters and me to understand how she could be so cheerful. It has dawned on me, though, that she was trying to make the best out of a no-win situation. Although she knew she was dying, she had the strength and the courage to celebrate life through laughter. This was eye-opening for me. I thought, if my mother could laugh under those conditions, what could be so terrible in my life that I couldn't do the same? From watching my mother, I learned that in almost every situation there is a way to find humor.

I am not suggesting we should be laughing at life's threatening issues, such as abuse, rape, murder, or other evils. There are times in life that call for stone-cold seriousness. What I am suggesting, though, is when you are faced with a crisis in your life, try to find a funny slant that will lift your spirits out of the doldrums. You will often find that when you can laugh out loud at whatever the problem is, the solution comes a lot quicker!

Another thing that was difficult for me to do was to learn to laugh at *myself*. Learning not to take yourself so seriously is the golden key that unlocks the door to emotional healing. One of my most sensitive issues is, as for many women, my weight. When I feel thin, I feel in control, as if I can conquer the world. When I feel fat, I get virtually paralyzed with fear, and I can't get out the door. I used to walk into my closet and feel like my clothes were out to get me. I used to think that in the middle of the night they all got together and shrank a few sizes, just to throw me off in the morning when I went to get dressed.

Sometimes I would feel so angry that I would throw a pair of pants across the room or slap them against the bed when they felt snug or the button wouldn't close. A friend of mine who happened to see me do this one morning started laughing hysterically. She said, "Do you think by slapping your pants on the bed and throwing them across the room, they will finally learn never to eat pizza again?"

I couldn't help but laugh at my bizarre behavior. It was ridiculous to beat up a pair of pants because I was a little bloated, but at the time all I felt was rage and anger toward myself. If my friend hadn't been there to interject humor into the situation, at that point in my life I could have done something destructive like make myself throw up or take too many laxatives. The humor put a whole different spin on the situation. Laughing at myself allowed me to forgive myself for eating a little too much the night before. I also realized that each day is a new day and I could assume a healthy eating and exercise regime.

The weight issue has been a struggle for me my whole life. As I get older, even though now I usually take good care of myself, it is harder and harder to maintain a good figure. However, these days I'm learning to approach my weight issue with acceptance and humor. As a result, I am so much more successful at winning the battle. I give myself permission to eat that chocolate cake once in a while. I know that it doesn't mean I will end up a fat, ugly slob no one can love.

Learning to see myself as a true human being who can't be "perfect" all the time was unbelievably liberating. Soon I was laughing at the parts of myself that made me feel ashamed. How can you expect others to like you if you don't like you? I began to find humor in the little oddities and quirks of my personality. I found that people were generally amused by me, not put off or disgusted. It was a great relief to see that people were laughing with me, not at me. I'm sure you will agree that it's the people who take themselves too seriously who end up the subject of ridicule. The people who can laugh about themselves are always endearing because everybody can relate to *not being perfect*. Aside from other people's perceptions, the main thing about laughing at yourself is for you to *like* yourself. I've spoken in great detail about self-love, but I've found it's also important to like who you are. The difference between self-love and liking yourself is simple. Self-love means self-acceptance. Liking yourself means you're enjoying it. It's important to like yourself because life can be really fun. The whole process of learning to both love and like yourself doesn't have to be all pain and drudgery. Give yourself permission to have a good time. This process is meant to lighten your life. Ask yourself the following questions.

Would you want to go to dinner with yourself? See a movie? Spend an afternoon just hanging out with yourself? These are questions I hope you would answer yes to. You can't really love yourself if you don't like yourself first. Humor can put you in touch with parts of yourself you can really get to appreciate. The self-discovery process doesn't have to be an arduous, painful, draining experience all the time. The whole objective here is to lighten up your life, not make it heavier.

Another area where laughter is important is in the realm of relationships, especially romantic ones. If a couple can laugh together, they have a much better chance of making it through tough times. Laughter also increases the bond between people. If two people can share a private joke or laugh at each other's "weirdness," they can begin to love, accept, and embrace the total uniqueness of each other.

Adding levity to a relationship also prevents people from getting bent out of shape over little things. As we all know, sometimes it's not just the big blow-ups that end a relationship. Sometimes it's a culmination of little irritating habits that bother you about your partner. One day, it just gets to be too much and you up and leave. Or even worse, he or she leaves you. I really believe if we could learn to laugh at the little things that bother us about a partner, and focus on the major things we really love about them, a lot of good relationships could be saved.

Humor makes you less judgmental. Being judgmental can be limiting because it closes you off from the people around you and what they have to offer. Sometimes our greatest teachers in life are the people we dislike the most. Again, this is where humor plays a pivotal role. If we can laugh with someone we originally thought we couldn't stand to be around, we know we have made real progress. Humor is the one thing we can count on to win us friends and disarm enemies. Although not everyone will get your jokes all the time, if you approach someone with the spirit of humor, you can't lose.

I believe that humor not only can save relationships, it can also do wonders to heal a broken heart. When a relationship comes to an end, it can often feel like a death, as I said before. When I broke up with my boyfriend of two and a half years, I had a really hard time finding humor in anything, let alone the erosion of the relationship. I was lucky to have my sisters and my girlfriends to make fun of him. Just as humor can help us highlight the good of our partners, it can comically exaggerate the bad when we need help letting go.

Making jest of my ex-boyfriend's need to eat extremely hot and spicy food was something we'd laugh about. We would imagine him pouring bottles of Tabasco sauce onto his new date's plate, and her being too polite not to try it. Then we would crack up thinking of how she would have to keep her composure as she started sweating, face all red and mouth on fire! I would also imagine him going into a very important business meeting after eating a jar of jalapeño peppers and beans—something he did often. I would laugh about how bad he could smell after such a meal and how oblivious he was to it.

These funny thoughts were not mean or destructive. They just helped me realize that he was not so perfect and I could get along fine without him. I never performed any of my comical fantasies I had, such as shaving his head while he was sleeping or slitting the back of all his pants. But just thinking about his reaction was enough to keep me rolling with laughter. The humor of these fantasies humanized him and knocked him off his pedestal in my mind.

I absolutely recommend to anyone going through a bad breakup to fantasize, visualize, and imagine your ex in comical, embarrassing situations. This is not vengeance, it's comic relief. By the same token, I absolutely in no way condone acting out or actually doing anything to harm or embarrass someone else, even an ex-partner who hurt you. Any destructive actions on your part will just make the situation worse for you. There is a huge difference between creating a comical fantasy in your mind and acting it out viciously. If you act destructively in any manner, you will look bad, feel worse, and make the situation more painful than it already is. Trust that everything ultimately works out for the highest good. That may be a harsh reality to deal with as you're going through a breakup, but in retrospect, most people are glad they've moved on to something better. Humor can make what seems like an eternity of unfairness go by a lot quicker. It's nature's best painkiller!

On the following pages are some exercises that will help you learn to laugh at yourself and the world around you. Take this opportunity to create and find humor in every aspect of your life. Go ahead, have a good giggle!

THE LAUGHTER SHEETS

1. What is the funniest situation you can remember being in? Who was there? Was it by accident or on purpose?

2. What was the funniest thing you ever did? Describe how you felt when you were able to generate laughter from those around you.

3. What was the funniest thing you ever said? Why was it so funny? Who heard it?

LAUGHTER SHEET

What are your favorite funny movies, and what makes them funny? Try to envision yourself as one of the characters in the funniest scenes you can remember. This will help you relate to yourself as a humorous human being. When faced with a crisis, think of how your favorite comedy character would handle it. Humor works wonders!

1. Funny movie: _____
   Your character is: _____
   Describe funny scene:

2. Funny movie: _____
   Your character is: _____
   Describe funny scene:

3. Funny movie: _____
   Your character is: _____
   Describe funny scene:

LAUGHTER SHEET

Now that you've got the hang of it, do the same for your three favorite TV shows.

1. Funny TV show:_____
   Your character is:_____
   Describe your favorite episode:

2. Funny TV show:_____
   Your character is:_____
   Describe your favorite episode:

3. Funny TV show:_____
   Your character is:_____
   Describe your favorite episode:

LAUGHTER SHEET

What are your three favorite jokes and what makes them funny? After you write down what they are on this page, use the next page to see if you can come up with three jokes of your own. Don't worry, they don't have to be funny to anybody but you. The purpose of this is to connect with the funny side of yourself that sometimes gets lost in the shuffle.

Favorite Joke #1:

Favorite Joke #2:

Favorite Joke #3:

LAUGHTER SHEET

Original Joke #1:

Original Joke #2:

Original Joke #3:

LAUGHTER SHEET

Hopefully, we all have people in our lives that make us laugh. If you don't have someone like this in your life, then I strongly suggest you go out and find a court jester! On this page list your three funniest friends or relatives and what you find funny about them. You may recall an amusing story you shared with them or a funny surprise they played on you. This will help you remember whom to call when you need a good laugh.

1. My funny friend's name is

_____

The funniest thing he/she has ever done is:

2. My funny friend's name is

_____

The funniest thing he/she has ever done is:

3. My funny friend's name is

_____

The funniest thing he/she has ever done is:

LAUGHTER AFFIRMATION

Ha!
When I was born
the world smiled
the heavens chuckled
and the earth roared.
I carry with me on my journey
that magic spark of lightness
which brightens up my path.
I laugh with the wind
and giggle with the sea
as I skip freely upon the waves
of my heart's innermost delight.
The joy within me
bubbles over with excitement
everywhere I go.
Laughter is my perfect way
to greet the universe
that winks at my wondrous notions
and grins at my gracious grandeur.
Ha Ha Ha Ha . . .

JODI LEVY

FIGHTING FEAR

For me the antithesis of humor is fear. This emotion, fear, can be one of the greatest obstacles to achieving total healing. Fear of something emotional or physical can stand in the way of one's progress. Fear can be paralyzing. It can prevent you from making real strides forward in life on a number of levels. Fear is the ultimate stifler of good, positive energy.

Believe it or not, there is good news about fear also. Fear can make you face your biggest challenges. Fear can motivate you to rise to the occasion and accomplish things beyond your wildest dreams. How can fear be a good and bad force at the same time?

Fear, to a certain extent, is natural. We are born with a "fight or flight" system that allows us to protect ourselves from danger. It is a natural part of our mental and physical makeup to want to survive. In a threatening situation, our adrenaline kicks in and we are given an energy surge to get us out of trouble. This is one example of how fear can serve us well.

It can also be put to good use when it drives us to achieve things out of the ordinary. A teenager who fears not getting into college may work extra hard to get good grades. That same teenager may stay away from drugs and away from gangs because he or she is afraid of going to jail. He or she may also practice safe sex or abstain in order not to contract a disease. Fear may stop you from getting behind the wheel of an automobile after a few alcoholic drinks because you don't want to get pulled over or get hurt. In these cases, fear acts as a positive force in people's lives.

However, when fear gets in your way and prevents true growth, it is a devil that needs conquering. I know a lot about fear. I used to be afraid of everything, especially myself. I didn't have many outwardly noticeable fears, like fear of flying or fear of heights. My fears were silent killers that made me my own worst enemy. I was afraid of losing control of my body by allowing myself to gain weight. I was afraid that because I came from the South and spoke with a Southern accent that people in New York would think I was stupid. I was also afraid that I *really was* stupid, and that people would find me a bore.

Starting my business helped me get over some of these fears. I knew that if I wanted to be successful, I had to talk to people. As I began to believe in my business concept, my confidence grew. As much as I love my family and friends, I have to honestly say, all of them were not one hundred percent behind my starting my own business. It's not that they didn't love me or didn't want me to succeed. I think, at the time, they thought it would be "too much" for me, or that I wouldn't stick with it. I don't really blame them for having their doubts. The old scared Jodi might have frozen up when challenges presented themselves, but I wanted so badly to make it work, I wouldn't allow myself to get overwhelmed. As things came up, I tried to handle each situation effectively, one by one. Pretty soon I realized I could do it, and the fear started to be replaced with gumption.

I remember when I started coming out with a holistic product line, and I wanted to get my candles, bath salts, and eye pillows photographed in some women's magazines. I was too intimidated to call the beauty editors, so I had my friend Mara do it. Once I saw how receptive the editors were to my products and how many magazines we were getting into, I began to feel comfortable talking about what I was doing. Today, Mara still calls the editors, but I have great relationships with most of them too. Now they call us to see what we're doing. I'm not trying to be immodest, I am just pointing out that if I can go from being too scared to speak to people to being interviewed in national magazines, so can anyone.

I also remember the first time I had to give a speech in public. It was at Gracie Mansion, the mayor's residence in New York City. My company, Healing Hands, was donating our first substantial check to the Susan B. Koman Foundation for Breast Cancer Research. It was a big early-morning press event. I had to get up in front of a room of journalists, the mayor, and CEOs from other companies that also supported breast cancer research and give a five-minute speech. Those were the longest five minutes of my entire life. When I got down off the podium, I saw the tears in my uncle Raymond's eyes. It was as if he couldn't believe that I was speaking in front of all those people.

At first, I couldn't believe it either. I thought there was absolutely no way that I could stand up and speak. The only thing that made me do it was my commitment to finding a cure for breast cancer. I missed my mother so much, I felt I owed it to her to do my part to fight this disease. My dedication to the memory of my mother gave me the courage to get out of my head of fears and into my heart.

As I stood up there speaking, something amazing occurred. All the so-called important people in the room became just plain *people*. I realized that although they had achieved great things in their lives professionally, we all still shared many of the same wants, hopes, dreams, and fears. There is really no reason to be scared of anybody else. Deep down, under all the pretense, we all need respect, and compassion. Not even the Queen of England can live without those things. On our core level, no matter what our position is in life, we share a common bond of loving and needing to be loved.

Fearing to love again after being hurt is also a big hurdle. In the laughter section I discussed some humorous ways I dealt with the breakup of my relationship. Even after I got over the pain and disappointment, the fear of loving someone again haunted me like an old ghost. This has taken me a long time to come to terms with.

It is just now, after totally hiding behind my work in the past few years, that I feel I can open myself up to someone on an intimate level again. For a long time, I had absolutely shut down. Fear stopped me from getting involved. Now, I feel like enough time has passed to put my fears of emotionally connecting with someone behind me. I learned that the breakup didn't kill me. It made me grow in a lot of ways. I couldn't permit fear to keep me isolated from the rest of the world anymore.

Socially, I am making strides. I am out there meeting people and going places. I feel comfortable talking to people I don't know at parties. I even manage sometimes to initiate conversations. This didn't happen overnight, but I just kept reminding myself of what I learned the day I spoke at Gracie Mansion. *People are just people!* We are here together to learn from one another and grow with each other. Rejection is nothing to be afraid of, really. If who you are or what you stand for doesn't work for someone else, then you are no less of a person because of it. Unfortunately, not everyone will share your vision.

The people who do gravitate toward you will see your greatness. If you get out of a place of fear and come from a place of courage and conviction, you're bound to win many more admirers. Just going along with the crowd because of fear of alienation will not get you the support you crave. I urge you to be a leader, and stand up for what is important to you in this world. Life is too short to just nod your head and accept everybody else's way of being.

Think of the people you look up to in your life. Think also about the people who have acted as role models for our society—Gandhi, Martin Luther King, Jr., and Abraham Lincoln, to name a few. These people didn't help to change the world by going along with the common viewpoint of their time. These people made a difference because their strength of will was greater than their fear.

Let me tell you a big secret. There is no difference between you and Gloria Steinem, or anybody else. I know this is hard to believe because we have canonized these people and put them on an unreachable pedestal. I'm certainly not belittling their life's work or diminishing the value of it by bringing them down to a human level. I am simply saying what I said before, and that is that people are really just people. If you want to achieve, contribute, or do something extraordinary in your lifetime, then don't let fear stand in your way. If you just want to be an "everyday superhero," then that is terrific also. What is an everyday superhero? It's a person who lives life according to ethical principles that don't hurt others and help them whenever possible.

An everyday superhero is the dad that takes all the kids on the block to movies on a Saturday afternoon. An everyday superhero is the friend you can call at three o'clock in the morning when you really need to talk to someone. An everyday superhero is the teacher in school who gave you a C on a paper because she knew that with just a little more effort you could get an A. An everyday superhero is a person who brings out the best in you because they are trying to be the best they can be. If everyone tried to be an everyday superhero, just think how much fun we'd have flying around in our capes and leotards making the world a more enjoyable place to be! Seriously, if just a little more than a few people were everyday superheroes, you would see a dramatic shift in the global consciousness of the human race. That may sound grandiose, but it's a simple truth. Think of what would happen if everyone did just one good deed every day. You be that everyday superhero.

FACING YOUR FEARS (1)

While you are in the process of becoming an everyday superhero, I challenge you to take on the fears that have stood in your path. You don't have to do this all at once. Pick one fear and really take it on. Once you have mastered it, go on to the next. This is also a process. You're not on a schedule. Just remember, the more courage you have to tackle your fears, the freer your life will be.

The following exercises will help you identify your fears and assist you in overcoming them. You're probably not alone in some of your fears. There are lots of people who share all different kinds of fears. It's up to you to be the one who gets over them. Make the decision and commit to it! Let's GO FOR IT! Nothing is totally impossible.

The only thing we have to fear is fear itself.
—*Franklin Delano Roosevelt*

FEARS BE GONE!

My name is _____
the Conqueror, and I am going to expel my fears from my
kingdom forever!

My biggest fears are:
1.
2.
3.
4.
5.
6.
7.
8.
9.
10.

EXAMINING MY FEARS

If you really think about it, there usually is a deep-seated reason that makes us afraid of something. Fears don't just happen by accident. If you stuck your hand in a fire, maybe you're now afraid of getting burned. Try to think about what experiences led to your fears. Whatever has been done, in time it can usually be undone. Use this page to recall the origin of your fears. Don't be afraid to reconnect with those initial feelings.

My fears come from:

PEOPLE I CAN DISCUSS MY FEARS WITH

If you have a best friend, favorite family member, or support group you can share you fears with, it can be of great help. You don't have to be afraid and alone anymore. You can always find a local support group in your area by asking friends, or relatives or even looking in the phone book. By getting together and "ganging up" on your fears, you have a much bigger fighting chance.

The people I can talk to about my fears are:
1.
2.
3.

They will understand and support me because:
1.
2.
3.

My favorite support group is _____
(This could be a group of friends, religious affiliation, family, group therapy, or twelve-step program.)

My support group helps me overcome my fears by making
me feel:

The people I will help in supporting to get over their fears are:
1.
2.
3.

FACING YOUR FEARS (II)

Now that you have identified your fears and have found people to share them with, it's time to do something about them! Let's get into action! On this page write down things that you can do to face your fears. If you are scared of flying, many airlines offer a "fear of flying" course. If you are afraid of heights, go a couple more stories higher than you would normally go in an office building. If you have a fear of public speaking like I did, gather a few friends together and tell them a story or a joke. Start by taking baby steps in the fearless direction. Pretty soon fear will be a thing of the past. Do something today!

Things I can do to face my fears:
1.
2.
3.
4.
5.
6.
7.
8.
9.
10.

A FEARLESS LIFE

On this page draw a picture of what your life would look like without your fears. Let yourself release your fears forever.

LIFE AT YOUR OWN PACE

Wherever you are in life, it's best when you are in forward motion. People who move upward and onward usually do so in their own time, at a pace that is challenging yet comfortable. Nobody really asks for big changes all at once. Yet those who find the fortitude to press on, reach for new goals, and search for new beginnings are so involved in the discovery of life that they forget their fears.

Fear is a paralyzing demon that halts the evolutionary process—a person's life flow. Fear can cause you to get stuck in a sedentary position, which stifles growth and development. When you face or conquer fear, you often find there was really nothing to be afraid of in the first place. The soul who rises above fear rises to the highest place beyond the heavens. The man who conquers his fears conquers many universes and shapes the world in which he dwells. Be a mover and shaker. Show fear the door.

THE FEARLESS AFFIRMATION

I am a member of a powerful universe and I am safe.
I have the courage to break through my boundaries
And move past my chosen limitations.
There is nothing that can hold me back
except my decision not to move forward.
I release the power that fear has over me.
I acknowledge that the power of my will is greater.
I deserve to win over my challenges.
Fear has no place in the motion of my life.
I am a person who has the confidence
and the eternal strength
to overcome any obstacles
that block my path.
I am my own leader.
I trust myself to make the right choices.
I know what's best for my life.
I have the power to make things happen.
I am in control when I need to be.
I am not afraid to let go.
My life works.

JUST YOU

Every one of us has been given certain obstacles to over-come. The challenges we face are a big part of the healing process because they build our character. Our character fortifies our spirit. Our spirit moves in sync with our body.

Those of us who have battled damaging addictions know all too well the toll they take on the mind, body, and spirit. Those of us who have faced serious illness are living proof of how recovery can be influenced by attitude and state of mind. Those of us who care for ourselves as a whole being, instead of just grooming the outside or treating a symptom, have health and prosperity in the long run.

Amidst the hectic schedule of your demanding life, love yourself enough to do something just for you. Don't think of it as being selfish. Think of it as loving and honor-ing yourself as you do others in your life.

138

HONORING MYSELF
WITH A WELL-EARNED TREAT

Circle your choice and add your own.

As a gift, I would most like
1.   a day or week at a spa
2.   a massage
3.   a piece of jewelry
4.   a naughty dessert
5.   a new outfit
6.   a vacation
7.   _____

My perfect day would be
1.   at the beach
2.   in the mountains
3.   spent shopping
4.   in bed with a lover
5.   reading
6.   on a boat
7.   _____

My favorite meal is

1. Italian casual
2. French bistro
3. Cajun
4. California trendy
5. Haute—or gourmet—cuisine, formal
6. _____

My favorite people are:

1. Mom
2. Dad
3. Sister
4. Brother
5. Lover
6. Best friend
7. Child
8. _____

THE PERFECT DAY

On this page create your perfect day. Let yourself have the best fantasy you can imagine. Remember that images are thoughts, thoughts are dreams, and if you will it, dreams can become your reality.

WHEN THE DAY IS DONE

As we conclude this healing journey, I'd like to thank you for allowing me the privilege of sharing this experience with you. I wish that at the end of your day you give yourself the gift of relaxation. For me, it was very hard to learn to wind down and shut off the noise in my head. I finally learned to quiet my mind. The meditations and the affirmation on the closing pages should help you ease into a comfortable state of rest.

On a personal note, I would like to congratulate all of you who are seekers of truth, happiness, and quality in your lives. I'm sure you have had to deal with challenges that have put every aspect of yourself to the test. I'm sure you have and will continue to come through with flying colors. There is one message I would like to leave you with to sum up the healing experience. That message is one of hope, self-love, self-worth, and total self-acceptance. Don't ever give up the quest for true contentment. You are here—we are all here—to live in the light of love. Thanks again for letting me be a part of your shining light!

EVENING MEDITATION

At the end of the day, sometimes we can't bring ourselves to unwind and shut out all the craziness from the world around us. It is crucial for us to be able to put the loud noise behind us so we can benefit from our well-deserved rest. To sleep in a total state of relaxation, we must make an easy, peaceful transformation from being "on" to a state of restful slumber. To help this process take place, start with this relaxation meditation and allow yourself to really settle down.

IN THE EVENING

The day is done.
I have worked hard.
I acknowledge that I have done my best
to contribute to an active, positive universe.
Now I deserve to rest.
I welcome sleep as my friend and comforter
and allow my energy to be recharged and renewed.
As I release my worries and troubles
I embrace the night gracefully,
As it drifts off into a peaceful state of bliss.
All is well in my world.
I let go of pain, problems, and challenges
to rejuvenate myself in a loving manner.
I wish for myself an undisturbed rest,
Full of beautiful dreams and visions
When my body sleeps
my soul reconnects with its universal love.
I allow myself the gift of sleep.
Good Night.

THE HEALING HANDS
DECLARATION OF
A DESERVING DESTINY

We at Healing Hands believe that
those who dwell on this earth
deserve the best possible destiny.
We acknowledge the responsibility and capability
to reach the destiny that
lies within each of us.
When we work through our fears,
care for our bodies,
and nurture our souls,
we know we are moving in an upward direction.
We also acknowledge the powers we gain
when we realize that the way we perceive life
is a result of our own choice.
We may not be able to control
everything all the time
but we have total mastery
over how we react to what is put on our plate.
We go forth
carrying the message
of Love, Light, and Joy
to all who come to know us.

JODI LEVY